MW00912051

Dedication:

This book is dedicated to my daughter Jacquelyn,
my favorite canoeing partner.
Tim Caverly

Text Copyright © 2009 by Tim Caverly
Illustrations Copyright © 2009 by Franklin Manzo, Jr.
All Rights Reserved. Published by Tim Caverly

Library of Congress Cataloging-in-Publication Data (PENDING)

Caverly, Tim.
    ALLAGASH TAILS: A collection of short stories from Maine's Allagash Wilderness Waterway
    Vol. I:
        A Merganser in the Allagash Wilderness Waterway/ by Tim Caverly;
        Illustrated by Franklin Manzo, Jr.
        p. cm. - (Marvin)
        "Tim Caverly"
    Summary: Marvin the Merganser is a fish eating duck who lives in the Allagash Wilderness Waterway in Maine. Marvin usually has very bad luck but his compassion for a neighbor changes all that.

        The White Water Beaver Of The Allagash/ by Tim Caverly;
        Illustrated by Franklin Manzo, Jr.
        p. cm. - (Charlie)
        "Tim Caverly"
    Summary: Charlie is a cross-eyed beaver with a narrow tail who dreams of a better life. See if he can overcome life's adversity in this charming "tail" for all ages.

    ISBN (PENDING)

Printed in the U.S.A.
First Printing, May 2009

11/6/2021

Enjoy!
Tim Caverly

Forward:

These two stories are the first in a series that are based on animal antics that we witnessed while living in the Allagash Wilderness Waterway.

The Marvin the Merganser tale was inspired one night while my family was sitting on the shore of Churchill Lake watching moose. We heard a strange noise, and in a short time a baby Merganser swam by with a clam closed on its bill. The duck was trying to quack with its mouth shut, and the sound was not like anything we had heard before.

The story about Charlie is based on a Beaver who, one summer, seemed to delight in living along Chase Rapids and swimming among the canoes.

I wish to thank my friends as well as the staff of the Millinocket Middle School who had the patience to help edit the stories. I also wish to thank Franklin Manzo, Jr. for his illustrations, and dedication that help make the stories come alive.

Tim Caverly
Millinocket, Maine

"MARVIN"
A MERGANSER IN THE ALLAGASH WILDERNESS WATERWAY

Follow a Merganser who usually has bad luck but his compassion for a neighbor changes all of that.

"MARVIN"
A MERGANSER IN THE ALLAGASH WILDERNESS WATERWAY

Did you ever have one of those days when everything seems to go wrong? Try as you might, no matter what you touch, no matter what you do, nothing goes right. Marvin was having one of those days. In fact, every day was one of those days for Marvin. Who is Marvin you ask? He is a duck. Not just any kind of duck but a particular species of duck. Marvin is a Common Merganser, also known as fish

eaters. That simply means that Mergansers have special teeth that allow them to catch and swallow small fish and other creatures that live in the water.

Even when Marvin was very small, his luck always seemed to be bad. He was the last of a family of ten to be hatched, and his brothers and sisters were always watching him and making fun of his misfortune.

It started the day Marvin broke out of his eggshell. The first thing that he saw was Melissa, the field mouse, eating seeds along the lake shore. Never having seen his parents before, Marvin thought the mouse was his mother.

"Hi Mom," he hollered.

Melissa couldn't believe her ears. "What was this duck doing calling her mother?" She had enough mouths to feed. In no uncertain terms, she told Marvin that she certainly was not going to take on another family member; especially one that wasn't any near as pretty as a mouse. Marvin's brothers and sisters couldn't believe that he would make the mistake of calling a rodent, mother. That was the first time they laughed at Marvin.

From then on things just kept going wrong for the Merganser. For example, there was the time a moose almost stepped on Marvin, and in trying to jump out of the way, Marvin fell into some moose droppings. Then, there was the time he tried landing on a wet boat dock. Tired from flying Marvin had spotted a boat dock on which he could rest. When his feet hit the dock, he slid across right off the other side and got caught on a nail driven into the side of the dock. Marvin hung in mid air from that nail for several hours until a friendly ranger came along and set him free. Things just always seemed to go wrong.

One particular day, Marvin had been eating fish in front of the fishway at Churchill Dam on the Allagash River. Marvin liked living on the Allagash and fishing in front of Churchill Dam. The fishway was an especially nice place to find a meal because that was the path fish used to swim from Heron Lake to the river. It provided easy food for a very lazy Merganser.

Marvin swam and ate, ate and swam. He thought, "This is so

easy." "I bet I could eat a whole meal with one-foot tucked under my wing. In fact, I think that I will just do that". Marvin tucked his right webfoot under his right wing. He caught a fish and felt really good about getting such an easy meal. Then all of a sudden, something terrible happened. The current was very strong on the downstream side of the dam, and Marvin had drifted into the current. Just as Marvin was about to grab another fish, a large wave whirled, twirled and swirled him around.

The current pulled Marvin along, all the time whirling, twirling and swirling. Marvin was getting dizzy. He had to get his foot from under his wing, so

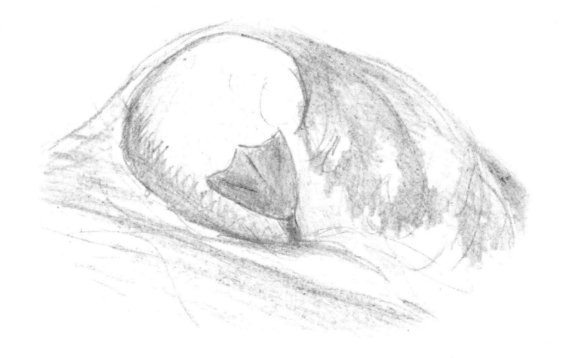

he could paddle straight and get to shore. But before he could get his foot free, the rapids had carried him over shallow rocks, "Oooh," said Marvin as his belly scraped, and he sucked in his breath. After pushing against the current, Marvin thought, "There has got to be calmer water. I am getting out of here for a while".

Marvin flew off to Churchill Lake with his nine brothers and sisters following. His brothers and sisters had gotten such a laugh from Marvin's latest trick that they couldn't wait to see what kind of trouble he was going to get into next. As Marvin flew over the dam, he could see Charlie the beaver eating alders along the bank of the river. After landing by the Jaws campsite on Churchill Lake, Marvin thought, "This is the life. Finally, calm water. No more rapids for me. Boy, all of that work has made me hungry."

Marvin landed on the lake and began fishing at once. He slowly cruised along near the shore with his head underwater looking for a tasty fish to eat. At times, he even swam completely under water, but there was just nothing to be found. Then, just as Marvin was ready to fly back to the fishway, he spied something on the lake bottom. Whatever it was, it looked good enough to

eat, and Marvin was really hungry. "This is more like it; lunch at last." Marvin dove to the bottom of the lake. Just as he reached to eat the tasty morsel, Marvin felt something clamp his bill shut.

"Thay, whath's going on?" Lisped Marvin.

"Hi, how are you?" Uttered the thing clamped on the end of Marvin's nose.

"Who are you and what are you doing to me?" Demanded Marvin.

"I am a clam," slimed the creature. "My friends call me Herb, but you can call me Herbert. After all, you were going to eat me."

"What do you want? Please get off my bill," pleaded Marvin. "You are hurting me." Marvin's brothers and sisters had lined up watching every minute, not believing what they were seeing, but at the same time they were excited to see what was coming next. This looked to be Marvin's best trick yet.

"I can't let go", said Herbert, "You see I need a ride."

"A what!" exclaimed a humbled Marvin. He had never even talked to a clam before much less given one a ride.

You know, a ride," said Herbert. "You remember that storm last week when the wind blew very hard from the south for several days?"

"Yeath," fumbled a frustrated and discouraged Marvin.

"Well, that storm," Herbert explained as he shed a little clam tear, "caused such turbulence and high waves that I was picked up and moved all the way across the lake. I was forced from my family. I've been here for five days, and I am getting awfully home sick."

Marvin was starting to feel so sorry for Herbert that he had forgotten that his bill was being pinched. Marvin offered, "How can I help?"

"Well, give me a ride back to my own clam bed, and I'll let go," said

Herbert. "By the way, near my home is good fishing in calm water, and it isn't very far."

"Ok," agreed Marvin, "let's get started! I am so hungry that I could eat a worm. The sooner we get there; the sooner I can eat."

Marvin's brothers and sisters had been listening. Although they had never seen anything like it, they were pleased to hear that Marvin was going to help a fellow Allagash neighbor. It was also good news to hear about the new place to fish. They couldn't make fun of him this time.

Marvin flapped his wings very hard and took off for Eagle Lake with the clam clenched on his bill. Marvin hollered, "Thang on, Herbert!"

Herbert replied, "Wow, I've never flown before, and what a view! Gosh, thanks for the ride," said Herbert as they neared his home. "By the way you can call me Herb."

Herb's family was happy to see him coming, and as Marvin landed, they clapped their little clamshells in appreciation of Marvin's efforts. Herb was reunited with his family, and Marvin had made a whole bunch of new friends. It was a very nice day for Marvin, a very nice day when everything had gone right.

THE END!

This story has received the Allie the Golden Retriever, Nose Touch of Approval

"CHARLIE"
THE WHITE WATER BEAVER OF THE ALLAGASH

Visit with an Allagash creature who, due to disabilities, has little confidence. But in a time of crisis he overcomes his impairment to help others and gains a new self respect.

"CHARLIE"
THE WHITE WATER BEAVER OF THE ALLAGASH

For as long as he could remember, Charlie, had not liked his name. The name Charlie just didn't sound important or worldly. He wanted his name to command respect; he wanted to be called something cultured like…… *Charles*. *Yes! That was it; Charles*. Charles had a much finer tone, and it sounded much more sophisticated than just plain old Charlie.

However, Charlie knew that his name would not be changed and that he could never be sophisticated. You see, Charlie was a beaver, and he knew that it was very difficult for a member of the rodent family to become elegant. He had been born to a proud beaver family and lived in a nice mud lodge on Heron Lake in the Allagash Wilderness Waterway. Though he enjoyed his life and loved his parents, Charlie thought he would be unsophisticated forever.

Even if a beaver could become gentlemanly, it became more difficult for such an animal to be accepted by others if he looked unusual. If he had something that others might see as an imperfection. The problem was that

Charlie had been cross-eyed and narrow tailed since birth. Just one of these defects is not good for a beaver, and Charlie had both.

Sure, Charlie had fine teeth. Sharp white teeth that could chew down a poplar tree in minutes. Always felling it in just the right spot for a dam. Sure, his fur was soft, and it kept him warm and dry in the winter and cool in the summer. But these were not enough. Charlie was cross-eyed. So cross-eyed that he saw two of everything and that caused him problems.

For example, just as Charlie would set his sights to bite into a tender poplar tree, he would miss and end up biting the tree growing beside it. Often that tree was a pitchy white pine. Now, as you probably know, the white pine has a pitch that has a terrible taste that can stick

to your teeth for days. Charlie always hated it when he bit into a pine by mistake. His beaver friends would always tease him and call him pine breath.

Another problem was his narrow tail. While most beavers have a beautiful wide leathery tail that can slap the water with a loud slap to signal danger, Charlie's tail was only two inches wide and six inches deep. It was not very useful. When Charlie tried to signal danger, his tail made a muffled thud, about the same sound as a small stick slapping a mud puddle. It was a very shameful tail for a full-grown beaver.

Although Charlie's house was on Heron Lake, several times a week he would swim to Churchill Dam and walk across the roadway to the Allagash River to eat a tender batch of alders. But Churchill Dam was another one of Charlie's problems. Not actually the dam itself, you see, but the gray steel wall that supported the dam. That darn steel wall! Sometimes canoeists would be at the dam when he wanted to cross, and they always made such a fuss and tried to pat him. Charlie liked people, and he liked to be petted.

"Look at the pretty beaver," the people would say. "What nice teeth.... look at his beautiful fur." But it was what came next that Charlie hated and hurt his feelings the most. "Why, he is cross-eyed! See the cross-eyed beaver! Look at his tail. It has such a funny shape. It is a lot narrower than a regular beaver's tail. What a strange sight… a cross-eyed, narrow tailed beaver!"

After that the people always laughed as they walked away from Charlie. *Why couldn't they take the time to get to know him? He was really a very nice fellow, if they would only say hello and maybe give him a pat on the head.* But the people always laughed, and it was very distressing for Charlie. Such talk always made him hurry across the dam's roadway a little faster. That was another problem. When Charlie walked too fast, it was hard for his eyes to focus. Hurrying only made his cross-eyed vision more blurred. Sometime when he hurried, he would miss the trail to the river and walk straight into the gray steel wall. When he hit the wall, he

always hit it with such force that he was knocked back onto his tail. That made the people laugh at him even harder. Every time it happened Charlie got very embarrassed, very embarrassed indeed.

One hot day in August Charlie was traveling from Heron Lake, across the roadway at Churchill Dam, to a cool pool of water at the head of Chase Rapids on the Allagash River. Just the day before Charlie had found a new bunch of alders. He thought he'd go back for a midmorning snack. As he crossed the road, he thought he could see two rangers giving instructions to people about how to canoe Chase Rapids. However, by the sound of the voice, Charlie knew there was only one ranger.

If only I weren't cross-eyed, thought Charlie. *Maybe I can sneak across while the ranger is keeping the canoeists busy. I don't want them to see me, and I don't want to be embarrassed again. I just can't stand to be laughed at another day.* Charlie scurried as fast as his stubby legs could carry him. He thought, *just a few more feet, and I'll be in the water where I can swim gracefully.*

Charlie almost made it when one of the humans hollered, "Look, look, everyone! See the pretty beaver, let's all go pat it."

Oh no, thought Charlie. He knew what was coming next. Sure enough it did.

"What a pretty animal. Wait; there is something wrong with it. Why, the beaver is cross-eyed and narrow tailed. Aren't beaver tails supposed to be wide?" The crowd all turned to look at Charlie. "Look how funny he walks! He is so cross-eyed that he can't see where to go. And his tail is so narrow it is leaving a gouge in the road dust. What a funny sight!"

Everyone started laughing.

How humiliating for Charlie. He knew better, but he was so embarrassed that he began scurrying away. He just had to get into the river and hide among the alders and grasses. Just as he was almost there, he stepped off the side of the dam and fell into one of the slippery spillways of the dam where the current was swift. Before he could say "munch a bunch", he was being flushed into the foaming, whirling rapids with such speed that he was dizzy with fear.

Now you probably realize that the rapids are fun for people who know how to canoe. But it isn't a fun place when someone accidentally falls into the whitewater. The whitewater especially isn't fun for a beaver that can't see very well, has a narrow tail, and is desperately flailing for calm water.

The strong current pushed Charlie down through the rapids. The beaver desperately tried to swim to shore where he would be safe and wouldn't have to hold his breath. The water was so swift that Charlie was beginning to give up any hope of making it to shore. He thought he was going to be forced to swim miles downstream all the way to the old Bissionette Bridge

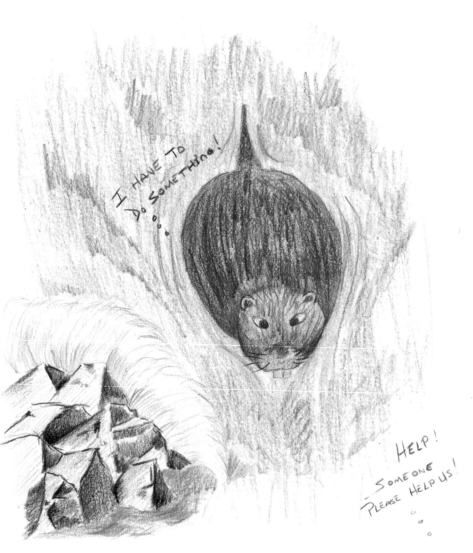

site. Suddenly he spied a canoe ahead in the river. Perhaps he could get a ride in the canoe and to safety. There was a man at the stern of the canoe and a woman in the bow. Wait, something was wrong! The woman was crying, and the man in the back was hollering. The canoe was starting to turn sideways in the current. It was out of control!

Charlie thought, *I must help, but what can I do? I am cross-eyed and narrow tailed. But, there must be a way I can help them!*

Charlie fought to regain control. Wait... but he was turning, how? Because his tail was narrow and deep, it worked better while swimming. He was able to use it like a rudder and steer. In fact, Charlie was able to steer very well. Charlie also realized that for every two rocks he saw, there was actually only one. So maybe, just maybe, if he aimed between the rocks, he could safely stay in the calmer channel of the river and reach the people before they capsized.

It worked! Charlie was amazed. *It worked*! He was swimming through the rapids, and it was even kind of fun.

The woman in the canoe saw Charlie and cried out, "Look at the beaver. Maybe we can follow him to safety."

Charlie glided gracefully through the current with the canoe following. Finally they were through the worst of the rapids, and everyone was safe. The people were very grateful for Charlie's help.

The lady reached down and scratched Charlie behind his ear. She said, "Thank you. Thank you for the help. Our canoe would have capsized without you."

Charlie was a proud beaver. But after such an adventure, it was time to go home to Heron Lake.

A little while later, an exhausted Charlie was crawling over the road at Churchill Dam

when he heard someone say, "Hey, everyone, look at the pretty beaver!"

Oh no, groaned Charlie, *I know what is coming next.*

This time, however, the people were not laughing. They were not making fun of him being crossed eyed and narrow tailed. The couple that had been in the canoe was in the crowd.

The man walked over to the beaver and said, "Hello Charlie."

The woman exclaimed, "No, you can't call him Charlie! He saved us when he could have only saved himself. After such an unselfish and gallant act, he needs a finer name; one that matches his beautiful fur and teeth. I know, we'll call him Charles."

Charles beamed. His dream of refinement was coming true. He was so happy that he walked a little straighter and held his head a little higher. Maybe he would be at the rapids again tomorrow to munch on a few twigs, and be ready to help in case someone else gets in trouble.

Charles was a very proud beaver as he sauntered back to his home. He thought, *who knows, maybe I'll show some of my beaver friends how to maneuver through white water. Why, yes! Maybe we will have a squad of ranger beavers who could travel the north woods helping canoeists.*

Charles had also noticed that the couple that he had helped was wearing glasses, he thought, *I wonder if they can make glasses for beavers that are cross-eyed?*

Pleased that he had overcome his disabilities and had helped someone, Charles slept very well that night, dreaming wonderful dreams about special abilities and making new friends.

THE END!

This story has received the Jasmine the Cat I don't really care look of boredom.

BE SURE TO LOOK FOR
MORE
"ALLAGASH TALES"...
VOL. II IS COMING SOON.